Dr. Roach

ISBN 978-0-545-42555-1

Text copyright © 2012 by Boxer Books Limited. Written by Paul Harrison. Illustrations copyright © 2012 by Tom Knight.

First published in Great Britain in 2012 by Boxer Books Limited. Based on an original idea by Sam Williams. Monstrous Stories™ concept, names, stories, designs, and logos copyright © 2012 Boxer Books Limited

12 11 10 9 8 7 6 5 4 3 2   12 13 14 15 16 17/0

Printed in the U.S.A.   40

First Scholastic printing, November 2012

The display type was set in Adobe Garamond.
The text type was set in Blackmoor Plain and Adobe Casion.

DR. ROACH'S
M🪳NSTROUS STORIES

ATTACK OF THE GIANT HAMSTER

SCHOLASTIC INC.

Contents

Dr. Roach Welcomes YOU!

Our story is about Hercules. No, not the mighty Greek hero — but a pet hamster called Hercules. He isn't strong. He is a small, fluffy, lazy little hamstery slob.

How amazing, then, that Hercules is able to scare the townsfolk, crush cars, and trample the farmers' market in search of some delicious food.

How you ask? Come closer, my friend, and I'll tell you all about it.

Welcome to Dr. Roach's Monstrous Stories. Enjoy!

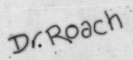

Chapter 1
Hairy, Fat, and Useless!

Hercules the hamster was quite possibly the world's laziest pet. Billy Philips sat in the living room, watching his hamster do what it did best — nothing. Billy had pestered his parents for ages for a hamster. Now that he had one, it was a massive disappointment. Hercules would sleep for most of the day and then occasionally wake up and waddle over to his food bowl. And that was as exciting as it got.

Billy reached into the cage and lowered Hercules onto his exercise wheel. Hercules sat there with a piece of lettuce sticking out of his mouth.

"Come on," said Billy. "Move."

Hercules stared at Billy, and slowly started chewing.

"You are a hairy, fat, useless slob," said Billy in disgust.

Hercules seemed to smile. Billy sighed and switched on the TV.

"Has your get-up-and-go got up and left?" said a voice on the TV. There was an image of an old lady snoozing in a chair. "Has all your vim vamoosed?" continued the voice-over man. "Then you need Booster Bites — the power snack that puts the power back!"

Now the old lady was bouncing across the screen.

"That's what you need, Hercules," muttered Billy.

"Try Booster Bites today, and if you're not happy we'll refund your money," the commercial promised.

Then it struck Billy — why not? Why not try feeding Hercules some Booster Bites? After all, if it didn't work, he could always get his money back. It was a brilliant idea! All the same, Billy thought he might not tell his parents about it just yet, in case they said no. Billy grabbed his jacket and raced down to the store.

Chapter 2
Booster Bites

When Billy got home, he crushed a couple of Booster Bites into some of Hercules's dry food. It didn't look very appetizing, so he chopped a bit of lettuce and cucumber into hamster-sized pieces and mixed those in, too.

"Perfect," said Billy.

He put it down next to Hercules.

"Lunchtime, Hercules!"

Hercules sniffed the bowl lazily. Then, to Billy's joy, he dug right in.

This is good. This is very good, thought Billy.

Billy sat and watched Hercules to

see if anything would happen. Hercules just sat in a little, fat, furry heap and stared right back.

Billy stared at Hercules.

Hercules stared at Billy.

Then Hercules fell asleep.

"Typical!" huffed Billy. He stomped away to the kitchen to make himself some lunch.

Billy wandered back into the room with a sandwich and a drink. He glanced over at Hercules — and stopped in his tracks! Was it his imagination or was Hercules bigger than before? Yes, yes, Hercules was definitely bigger and awake.

Billy did a little jig of delight, but stopped very quickly. Hercules had grown again. The hamster was now three times his normal size.

A terrible thought struck Billy: How would he explain this to his parents? He began to panic.

He looked at Hercules again — he was still growing. There was no other choice — Billy had to hide him. Billy scooped up the cage and charged upstairs. Then he wondered what to do next.

Chapter 3
Panic!

In a panic, Billy dashed back to the kitchen and grabbed the box of Booster Bites. Frantically, he read the back, looking for something that might explain what was happening to Hercules. Nothing — but there was a telephone number for customer service.

Billy dialed the number. "Hello, Booster Bites customer service, how can I help you?" said a woman's voice.

"Hi," Billy replied, "I think your Booster Bites are making my hamster grow."

"You fed them to your hamster?" the woman said.

"Ummm, yes . . ."

"And they're making it grow?"

"Yes," Billy replied.

"Well, Booster Bites are a nutritious snack . . ."

"My hamster is three times his size! And he's still growing!"

"Oh. Well, we don't recommend that Booster Bites are fed to animals," said the woman.

"It doesn't say that on the package!" said Billy, panicking.

"Really? Are you sure your hamster is actually growing? It hasn't just fluffed its coat up a bit?" said the woman.

"Fluffed up? He looks like a hairy balloon!" said Billy.

"Is this some kind of joke?"

"No, no, no; something is wrong with my hamster," said Billy.

"Hmm. Well, I suppose we could send a scientist down to have a look tomorrow. . . ." The woman sounded doubtful.

"Great, thank you, thank you, thank you!"

Before the woman could change her mind, Billy gave her his address and hung up.

Chapter 4
Hamster Dung

Knowing help was on the way made Billy feel better. He dashed back upstairs to check on Hercules. That made him feel worse. Hercules had gotten so big he burst out of his cage. Where could Billy hide him now? Billy raised his eyes upward, searching for inspiration. And there it was, right above him — the attic!

The only way Billy could get him up the ladder was to put Hercules over his shoulder, like a really heavy beanbag.

Billy just got the attic door closed when his parents arrived home.

"Hi, Billy, we're back. Everything okay, sweetie?" called his mother.

"Sure . . . fine, Mom," Billy replied, casting a nervous glance upward.

❋❀❋❀❋❀❋❀❋

The rest of the day was difficult. Hercules continued to grow. By the afternoon, he was the size of a cow. The bigger Hercules got, the hungrier he seemed to be. Billy had to smuggle more and more food up to the attic.

However, there was a bigger and smellier problem. A huge Hercules had massive poos.

"And I thought cleaning your cage out was bad," grumbled Billy as he shoveled great lumps of hamster dung into garbage bags.

Hercules just looked at Billy and chomped down another head of lettuce. The poo couldn't stay in the attic. Billy had to carry it downstairs and flush it down the toilet. All these trips to the bathroom were not going unnoticed.

"You feeling okay, sweetie?" his mom asked.

"I'm fine, Mom," Billy lied.

By bedtime, the toilet was clogged. As Billy's dad, Herman, struggled to unclog the toilet, he grumbled about how much a plumber would cost. Billy counted down the hours until tomorrow.

Chapter 5
Professor Heinzwinkel

The new day brought more bad news. The ceiling above Billy's bedroom was bulging downward. How long would it be before his parents noticed? Billy wondered. But luckily, they were too busy wondering why the refrigerator was empty.

"What have you done with all the carrots, Herman?" asked Billy's mom.

"Carrots? What carrots?" replied Billy's dad.

"The lettuce is gone, too!" yelled Billy's mom. "Any ideas, Billy?"

"Um . . ." Billy tried to think of something to say.

Ding-dong! There was someone at the door.

He was saved by the bell.

"Ah, that must be the plumber," said Billy's dad, going for the door.

"Good morning, my name is Professor Eric von Heinzwinkel," said the visitor.

"Professor? That's very educated for a plumber," said Billy's dad.

"Plumber? No, I'm here about the hamster," replied the professor.

"Hamster?" said Billy's dad.

"He's come to see Hercules," said
Billy, taking the professor by the arm
and dragging him upstairs.

"Am I glad to see you!" said Billy.

He opened the attic door, but they
couldn't get in because Hercules was
filling the entire space.

"Billy! What's going on up there?"
his dad called.

Ding-dong!

Once again, the doorbell came to the rescue.

"Are you another professor?" asked Billy's dad.

"No, I'm a plumber. But I reckon you need someone to fix your roof."

"What's wrong with the roof?" said Billy's dad.

Just then a roof tile smashed to the ground.

Billy's mom and dad raced outside. Tiles were falling off the roof and ginger fur was poking out.

"BILLY!"

shouted his dad.

Chapter 6
Falling Down

CREAAAAKKKKKK!
GRRRROOOAAAAANNNNN!

Billy and the professor charged out of the house — right into Billy's parents and the plumber.

"Billy Philips, I demand to know

what's going on — right now!" shouted his dad.

"I . . . well . . . it's d-d-ifficult to explain. . . ." stammered Billy.

"Try me," his dad replied.

Just then a massive crash came from the house.

"What in the world was that?" said Billy's mom.

"I'll help pay for any damage!" cried Billy.

The house began to shudder.

Billy, his parents, the plumber, and the professor moved farther away from the house. Hercules had just crashed through the ceiling and was growing at an enormous rate. With a terrible crunching sound, the walls of the house were pushed out and came crashing to the ground in a massive cloud of dust.

"Billy," said his dad, "on your current allowance, you'll be paying for this damage until the year 3000."

The dust slowly cleared, revealing a giant-size Hercules sitting where the house used to be.

The roof sat on Hercules's head at a stylish angle like a hat. The hamster blinked a couple of times, as if it had just woken up, and yawned. It shook itself free of the mass and started munching on the plants in the Philipses' garden.

"That . . . that . . ." Billy's mother struggled to find the right words.

". . . is Hercules," said Billy.

"Do I take it you don't need me anymore?" said the plumber — and, without waiting for an answer, he ran for his van.

"I'd better go, too," said Professor Heinzwinkel. "I need to get some stuff from my lab. I'll be back as soon as I can. Don't let him out of your sight."

"Well, that's unlikely," sa
dad. "Look at the size of him!

Just then, Hercules sniffed the
something had gotten his atten
Abruptly, he got up and waddled
down the street, squashing cars and
knocking over streetlamps as he went.

ere's Hercules going?" shouted

ly's dad.

"He's heading for town," cried Billy.

"Of course! THE FARMERS' MARKET!" wailed his mom.

For a moment, the Philipses stopped and thought about what would happen when a huge, hungry hamster came face-to-face with a market stuffed with its favorite food. It was not a pleasant thought — unless of course you were a hamster. Then it was the stuff of dreams. . . .

Chapter 7
Call the Army

Hercules could hardly believe his pudgy cheeks when he saw all the vegetables. The people in the market couldn't believe their eyes when they saw a sixty-foot-tall hamster descending on them.

"ARGGGHGHHH!" they cried and scattered in all directions. Hercules ignored them and filled his face with food.

By the time the Philips family arrived, Hercules had eaten everything in sight and was settling down for a lengthy snooze.

"What now?" asked Billy's dad.

"We wait for the professor," said Billy.

"Excuse me, is that your hamster?"

Billy turned around. There was a police officer standing there.

"Yes, that's my pet, Hercules," Billy replied.

"You've got some explaining to do, son."

While Billy tried to explain the unexplainable, a lot was going on.

First the police roped off the area to keep people away. Then, as night fell, helicopters whirred overhead and there was a rumble of trucks and tanks as the army circled the area.

"What's going on?" Billy asked, turning to his dad.

"It's Hercules, son," his dad replied. "The army is going to deal with him in the morning."

"No one's shooting my pet!" shouted Billy. He ducked under the police rope and went straight to the general leading the army.

"You can't do this," said Billy.

"Oh, yes we can, sonny," the general replied.

"But the professor is coming with a cure!" Billy pleaded.

The general looked at his watch.

"How long will your hamster sleep for?" asked the general.

"Normally until breakfast time," Billy replied.

"Well, then," the general said. "Your professor has got until 7:30 A.M. to get here. If he's not, then we go in."

Chapter 8
Hold Your Nose!

It was a warm night, so Billy, his mom, and his dad all spent the night nearby in a police tent with police sleeping bags. But Billy didn't sleep a wink. This was partly from worry, but mainly because Hercules had been snoring. Billy wasn't the only one kept awake. The general was pacing up and down by the rope in a foul temper.

"We can't risk the hamster waking up — I'm sending in the troops now."

"But it's only seven o'clock!" shouted Billy.

"Hello, hello, good morning!" said a new voice.

"Who on earth . . . ?" said the general.

"I am Professor Heinzwinkel. Hello, Billy — glad to see you kept an eye on Hercules for me. Now, not a moment to spare. Pop this pill into Hercules's mouth."

The professor gave Billy a large tablet. Billy put a head of lettuce around it, raced straight over to Hercules, and slipped it into the hamster's mouth.

"What happens now?" asked Billy.

"I'm not entirely sure. . . ." the professor admitted.

For a moment, nothing happened. Then Hercules opened his eyes wide, looking alarmed. He began to get bigger and rounder by the second.

"He's growing again," cried the general. "I'm sending in the tanks!"

"No, wait!" said the professor. "It's the tablet working. It's turning all the growth into gas."

Hercules now looked like a giant, furry soccer ball.

"But how will the gas get out?" asked Billy.

"One of two ways . . ." the professor began.

Hercules's body tensed up and his eyes crossed. Then, with a mighty toot, he shot into the air like a rocket.

Hercules sped this way and that through the sky like a balloon that had been let go.

He crashed into a cell-phone tower and bounced off buildings, all the while getting smaller and smaller.

After a minute or so, he was back to normal size and fell gently down toward the ground, where he was caught by a grateful Billy.

"Good, good, good," said Professor Heinzwinkel. "Everything is back to normal."

"Thanks, Professor!" said Billy. "From now on I'll try not to care how lazy Hercules is!"

"Yes, just keep him off the Booster Bites and all will be good."

And everything did feel good. Apart from the damaged buildings, and the flattened street lamps, and the crushed cars, of course.

Oh yes, and the terrible smell of hamster gas.

HURRY!

Do you have a favorite place? Sammy and Tammy do. They love the quiet Boggy Marshes near their home. They're full of insects and strange plants.

Meet Maximus Sneer. An evil man with lots of money and a secret plan. He plans to drain the Boggy Marshes dry and cover them with houses, stores, and parking lots.

But instead of creating homes, he creates two giant monsters — without even knowing it.

How you ask? Get a copy today and I'll tell you everything!

Catch you later!

Dr. Roach